What Do You Find in a Pond?

Megan Kopp

Crabtree Publishing Company
www.crabtreebooks.com

Ecosystems Close-Up

Author
Megan Kopp

Publishing plan research and development
Reagan Miller

Editors
Janine Deschenes
Crystal Sikkens

Design
Ken Wright
Tammy McGarr (cover)

Photo research
Janine Deschenes
Crystal Sikkens

Production coordinator and prepress technician
Ken Wright

Print coordinator
Katherine Berti

Photographs
iStockphoto: cover
Thinkstock: page 22
Wikimedia Commons: Guitardude012: page 12 (inset)
All other images from Shutterstock

Library and Archives Canada Cataloguing in Publication

Kopp, Megan, author
    What do you find in a pond? / Megan Kopp.

(Ecosystems close-up)
Includes index.
Issued in print and electronic formats.
ISBN 978-0-7787-2259-5 (bound).--ISBN 978-0-7787-2279-3 (paperback).--
ISBN 978-1-4271-1724-3 (html)

    1. Pond animals--Juvenile literature. 2. Pond ecology--Juvenile
literature. I. Title.

QH541.5.P63K67 2016   j591.763'6   C2015-907990-X
                                     C2015-907991-8

Library of Congress Cataloging-in-Publication Data

Names: Kopp, Megan, author.
Title: What do you find in a pond? / Megan Kopp.
Description: New York, New York : Crabtree Publishing Company, [2016] |
   Series: Ecosystems close-up | Includes index.
Identifiers: LCCN 2015047295 (print) | LCCN 2015047593 (ebook) | ISBN
   9780778722595 (reinforced library binding) | ISBN 9780778722793 (pbk.)
   | ISBN 9781427117243 (electronic HTML)
Subjects: LCSH: Pond animals--Juvenile literature. | Pond ecology--
   Juvenile literature. | Ponds--Juvenile literature.
Classification: LCC QL146.3 .K67 2016 (print) | LCC QL146.3 (ebook) |
   DDC 578.763--dc23
LC record available at http://lccn.loc.gov/2015047295

Crabtree Publishing Company

Printed in Canada/032016/EF20160210

www.crabtreebooks.com   1-800-387-7650

Published in Canada
Crabtree Publishing
616 Welland Ave.
St. Catharines, Ontario
L2M 5V6

Published in the United States
Crabtree Publishing
PMB 59051
350 Fifth Avenue, 59th Floor
New York, New York 10118

Published in the United Kingdom
Crabtree Publishing
Maritime House
Basin Road North, Hove
BN41 1WR

Published in Australia
Crabtree Publishing
3 Charles Street
Coburg North
VIC 3058

Contents

What is a Pond?

Ponds are small, shallow areas of fresh water. They are bigger than a puddle, but smaller than a lake. Most ponds are filled by a river or by rainfall. Some ponds are human-made.

*Some ponds are created when a beaver **dam** holds water back.*

Pond Life

Many different kinds of plants and animals live and grow in and around ponds. Plants such as cattails are often found growing in a pond. Many kinds of insects, birds, and animals build their homes in the water or on the land around ponds.

5

A Pond Ecosystem

A system is made up of connected pieces that work together. Each piece has a role to play. If any piece of the system is missing, the system will not work as it should. **Ecosystems** are types of systems. They are made up of all living and nonliving things found in one place.

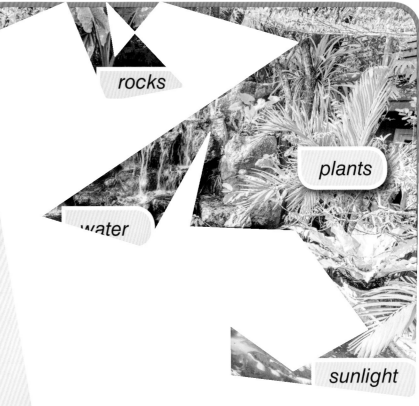

rocks

plants

water

sunlight

What do you Think?

Look at this picture. Can you name the living and nonliving things found in this pond ecosystem?

6

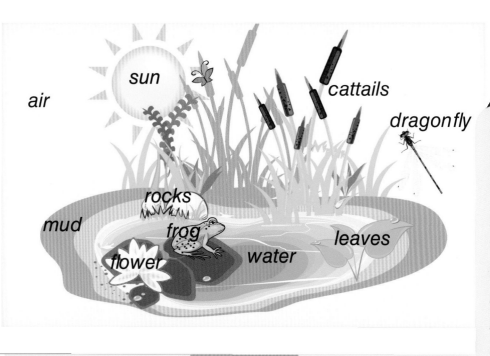

air

sun

cattails

dragonfly

rocks

mud

frog

flower

water

leaves

Scientists use **models**, such as this computer diagram of a pond ecosystem, to help them understand how living and nonliving things are connected.

A System that Works

All of the living and nonliving things in a pond ecosystem are connected. Plants and animals are living things. Living things change as they grow. They make new living things. Plants create new plants. Animals have babies. Nonliving things, such as air and mud, are not alive. They cannot grow or change.

Life in a Pond

Plants and animals need both nonliving and other living things in order to **survive**, or stay alive. Plants need water, air, and sunlight to make their own food. The food gives them **energy** to grow.

Some animals, such as beavers, eat plants to stay alive.

Meeting Needs

Animals need water, air, food, and shelter to survive. Plants and animals can live only in ecosystems where they have everything they need.

Frogs often use pond plants, such as water lilies, for shelter.

What do you Think?

Name three things that both plants and animals need in order to survive.

Food Means Energy

Living things need food to survive. Plants make their own food using sunlight, air, and water. Ponds are open areas with a lot of sunlight and water. This allows a lot of plants to grow and survive near ponds.

Algae are small plants that can cover large areas of water in ponds.

Time to Eat!

Animals cannot make their own food. They get energy from eating other living things. Some animals eat pond plants. Snails eat algae. Some animals only eat other animals. Frogs eat animals, such as snails and insects, to get the energy they need. A **food chain** shows how energy moves from one living thing to another.

snail

algae

What do you Think?

If there were no algae in a pond, would the ecosystem change? How?

This picture shows an example of a pond food chain. The arrows show the flow of energy.

Breathe Deep

All living things need air to live. Air is a nonliving thing. It is all around a pond ecosystem. Insects such as dragonflies breathe through small holes along the sides of their bodies. Beavers take in air above the water with their lungs.

gills

Fish, tadpoles, and other animals use **gills** to breathe underwater.

Drink up!

Young frogs are called tadpoles. They live in the water and breathe using gills. Tadpoles change as they become adult frogs. They grow legs and move onto land. Their gills are replaced with lungs to breathe air above water.

Tadpoles have tails. As they grow, their tails slowly shrink. They no longer have tails when they become adult frogs.

tadpole

adult frog

The Watering Hole

All plants need water to make their own food. Some plants float on the surface of a pond and have roots at the bottom that soak up water and **nutrients**. Other plants live on or underneath the water. They soak up water through their leaves.

Water lilies are common pond plants. Their floating leaves are held in place by a long stem attached to roots at the bottom of the pond.

stems

This green frog is soaking up water as it sits in its pond ecosystem.

Belly up!

Frogs, toads, and salamanders lay their eggs in water. They drink with their skin rather than their mouths. Frogs and toads have a patch of skin on their bellies that they use to soak up the water they are sitting in.

What do you Think?

What would happen to the pond ecosystem if the water disappeared?

A Case for Shelter

Animals in ponds depend on living and nonliving things for **shelter**. A shelter is a safe place that can hide them from other animals that want to eat them. Some insects build shelters in dead wood or rocks. Beavers use tree branches to build their shelters.

This wasp is an insect that builds its shelter underground.

This mother swan has had babies in the nest she built among the tall plants of a pond.

Many uses

A shelter is also a place to lay eggs or have babies. Ducks build nests in the ground at the edge of ponds. Tall plants help hide the nest from other animals. The ducklings also use the water to get to and from the nest.

Disappearing Act

Wetlands are areas where there is a lot of water in an area of land. They have holes that become ponds when water fills them. They are important ecosystems for many types of animals. These areas are in trouble.

These California wetlands are dried up. Living things that depend on water can no longer survive here.

What do you Think?

What might happen to a pond ecosystem if pollution made the water dirty?

Drained, polluted, and dry!

Many small ponds are drained for farming, or to build towns and cities. Weather changes can also cause small ponds to dry up. Ponds can be easily damaged by pollution. Pollution is human-made waste that hurts pond ecosystems.

Make a Model

We use models to help us understand how different things are connected. A model is a **representation** of a real object. Pictures, storyboards, **dioramas**, maps, and diagrams are all kinds of models. You can create your own model of a pond ecosystem. Follow the instructions on the next page to make a diorama of a pond in a jar.

Materials you will need:

- jar with tight-fitting lid
- small rocks, plastic frogs, rubber fish, rubber water insects, and water plants
- blue food coloring
- water
- small cardboard or paper pictures of birds, animals, and nonliving things, such as the Sun.
- tape or glue

Creating a pond ecosystem diorama

1.   Carefully pour the water into your jar. Put a few drops of blue food coloring into the water. Ask an adult to help with this step.

2.   Build the inside of your pond by putting rocks and plastic plants and animals into your jar.

3.   Tape or glue cardboard or paper animals, plants, or nonliving things to the outside of the jar.

21

Dive in a Little Deeper!

Scientists use models to help them learn more about the systems they study. Now, it is your turn!

Present your diorama to family and friends. Help them understand how your pond ecosystem meets the needs of the different plants and animals included in your model.

What do you Think?

How do the living and nonliving parts of your pond ecosystem work together?

Learning more

Books

Hawthorne, Jane. *A Frog Named Lilly The Amazing Adventures of a Pond Frog* (The Life Cycle of Animals-Frogs Book 2 – Kindle edition), Amazon Digital Services, Inc., 2015.

Wallace, Nancy Elizabeth. *Pond Walk*. Two Lions, 2015.

West, David. *Nora the Naturalist's Animals: Pond Life: 2.* Franklin Watts, 2015.

Websites

Earth Kids: Ponds and Wetlands Science
http://www.earthskids.com/ek_science-pond-wetland.htm

BBC Schools Science Clips
http://www.bbc.co.uk/schools/scienceclips/ages/8_9/habitats.shtml

Easy Science for Kids: Lakes and Ponds
http://easyscienceforkids.com/all-about-lakes-and-ponds/

Wartgames: Build Your Own Pond
http://www.msnucleus.org/membership/activities/pond2.html

Words to know

algae (AL-jee) noun Small plants without roots or stems that grow mainly in water

dam (dam) noun A barrier that stops the flow of water

diorama (dahy-uh-RAM-uh) noun A three-dimensional display or scene representing something real

ecosystem (EE-koh-sis-tuhm) noun All the living things in a place and their relation to the environment

energy (EN-ur-jee) noun The ability to do things

food chain (food cheyn) noun The order of living things in an ecosystem by which food energy is passed from one to another

gill (gil) noun A special body part which allows fish to breathe underwater

model (MOD-l) noun A representation of a real object

nutrient (NOO-tree-uh-nt) A substance that living things need to grow and stay healthy

representation (rep-ri-zen-TEY-shuh n]) noun A picture, drawing, model, or other copy of something

shelter (SHEL-ter) noun The place where living things are safe

survive (ser-VAHYV) verb To stay alive

A noun is a person, place, or thing. A verb is an action word that tells you what someone or something does.

Index